D0461125

The Christmas Bus

by Robert Inman

Illustrations by Lyle Baskin

NOVELLO festival PRESS

CHARLOTTE 2006

Library of Congress Cataloging-in-Publication Data

Inman, Robert, 1943-
  The Christmas bus / by Robert Inman; illustrations by Lyle Baskin.
      p. cm.
   Summary: Worried that the Trustees will oust her as director of
  Peaceful Valley Orphanage, Mrs. Frump tries to make Christmas
  unforgettable for the eight orphans known as The Hooligans, while a
  singer from a nearby town must decide between staying home and
  seeking his fortune.
   ISBN 0-9760963-6-6 (hardcover)
   [1. Orphans—Fiction. 2. Christmas—Fiction. 3. Singers—Fiction.]
  I. Baskin, Lyle, ill. II. Title.
  PZ7.I573Chr 2006
  [Fic]—dc22

2006017582

© 2006 by Robert Inman

Published in the United States by Novello Festival Press, Charlotte, North Carolina.

This is a work of fiction and any resemblance to real persons or events is purely coincidental.

Printed in the United States of America
FIRST EDITION
Book design by Bonnie Campbell

★ ★ ★ For Lee and David Farabaugh ★ ★ ★

1 ✳ The Orphanage

Not so very long ago and not so very far away, there was a place called Peaceful Valley. It was a green and pleasant place, with orchards and pastures and farmland, vegetable gardens and sturdy barns, and a dusty road meandering from one end to the other. But Peaceful Valley was not exactly a peaceful place, and the reason was the Peaceful Valley Orphanage.

The orphanage sat atop a small rise in the middle of the valley—a sagging white frame house with shutters askew and paint flaking from its weary sides. It had the rather desperate look of an old shoe that has been worn too long and is in great need of either repair or the trash can.

Its residents were known far and wide as the Hooligans. They were an energetic and rambunctious collection of young people, given to high jinks and mischief.

There were four girls: Clara, Hilda, Jenny, and Louann. Clara was the oldest, fifteen or thereabouts, and though she could be just as rowdy as the rest when it came time to play, she was also a motherly type and helped take care of the younger children. Hilda was twelve, just beginning to be interested in boys and makeup, both of which frequently landed her in the doghouse. Jenny was ten, a sweet-tempered girl who nevertheless enjoyed a good romp and had a voice that could make the windows rattle when she was especially happy or bothered. Louann was the smallest and youngest of all the children, and frequently referred to by the others as "the munchkin."

Eighteen-year-old Thomas was the oldest of the four boys. More about Thomas in a moment. Frankie was next, but among all the children, the most likely to dream up mischief and then to be the ringleader of some especially mischievous act. Everything from his slightly crooked grin to his constantly moving feet said that he would do something daring at the drop of a hat and then dare you to catch him. Eugene was perhaps the brightest of the bunch, a fine student of cause and effect. Eugene was forever trying something new, like jumping from the roof of the orphanage to see what it would be like to land in the nandina bush below. You could usually tell Eugene immediately among the children, because he was the most likely to wear a cast or bandage as a result of some mishap.

And then there was Donald, who was a fairly recent arrival, and his constant companion, a potted geranium plant. There had been a fire at Donald's home awhile back, and Donald and the geranium were the only survivors. A sad story. But Donald was doing okay at the orphanage. The other kids were kind and understanding, and nobody paid much attention to the fact that he carried that geranium around all the time. The unwritten rule at Peaceful Valley was that you just accepted everybody as they were, geraniums and all.

So those were the Hooligans, and they pretty much lived up to their name. On most days, the orphanage wavered between chaos and confusion, with a little hullabaloo thrown in for good measure.

The only thing that kept the place from completely coming apart at the seams was Mrs. Frump. The kids called her simply "Frump." She was officially known as the Director of the Orphanage, but Director didn't nearly describe what she did or what she meant to the residents. She was mother, cook, nurse, tutor, wiper of noses, soother of hurt feelings, and all-around Number One Fan of her children. She had been at the orphanage for many years, and sometimes it seemed that she was on the verge of a nervous breakdown. Her favorite cry was "It's a madhouse!" But she was a kindly and optimistic soul. The kids loved her and called her a Good Egg. She gave big hugs, tucked every child into bed every night, darned their socks when they got holes in them, didn't raise a fuss when somebody spilled his milk, and kept her apron pockets full of jellybeans.

Frump's right-hand man, her trusted assistant, was Thomas, the oldest of the orphans. He had been at the orphanage almost as long as Frump. She found him one morning on the doorstep: a little baby, wrapped warmly in a blanket, in an apple crate. Over the years, most of the kids who came to the orphanage stayed for a while, then went on to good, permanent homes. But for some reason, nobody took Thomas.

So he stayed, growing up and helping Frump. Thomas was a smart and clever young man, a whiz at things mechanical and electrical. He could take apart a broken lawnmower or kitchen appliance, figure out what was wrong, and have it back together and working properly in a jiffy, even without written instructions. In a few months, he'd be graduating from high school, and wanted to become a mechanical engineer.

Frump marveled at Thomas's intelligence and cleverness. She was forever admiring his work—for instance, the day she found him hunched over his desk, drawing intricate lines and angles and shapes on a piece of paper. "What's that you're working on now, Thomas?" she asked.

"A kid-o-mometer," he said. "See," he showed her on the drawing, "you put a dirty, hungry kid in this end about five o'clock in the afternoon, press a button, and he comes out the other end at six: clean, fed, and with his teeth brushed."

"What on earth will you think of next!" Frump exclaimed. (She was a woman of great enthusiasms, and was constantly exclaiming about one thing or another.) "One of these days, I'll be telling the children, 'If you study hard in school, you'll be a big success like our illustrious Thomas—Doctor of Mechanical Engineering, and winner of the Nobel Prize for Thing-A-Ma-Jigs.'"

"You'll be my special guest at the award ceremony," Thomas said with a grin. And then his grin faded. "But that means I've got to go to college, and there's no money for college. I'll graduate from high school and get a job at Dub's Garage and spend my life rebuilding carburetors and patching tires."

"Nonsense," Frump said. "We'll find a way, I'm sure of it. I've got faith in you, Thomas, and you must have faith in yourself."

There was, indeed, no money for college educations at the Peaceful Valley Orphanage, or for much else, for that matter. Frump had to make do on a very limited budget and the goodness of people who lived in the nearby town. But she patched and mended, scrimped and saved, and served gallons and gallons of stir fry for dinner each week. The kids moaned and groaned about all that stir fry, but it was chock full of good vegetables and occasional bits and pieces of chicken and beef, and it quite nicely filled up young stomachs at dinnertime. During the warm months, Frump and the orphans planted and tended a large and bountiful garden and their stir fry had plenty of fresh vegetables. What was left over, Frump put in jars to last through the winter. When the kids groaned over their stir fry on a cold January night, they sometimes wished that garden hadn't been so large or bountiful.

2 ❋ Visitors

There were occasional visitors to the orphanage, and the most frequent was Sheriff Snodgrass. He often stopped by for a helping of Frump's famous apple cobbler, but there was often business to transact, too.

For instance, there was the autumn day when he arrived with the mischievous young Frankie in tow and knocked on the orphanage front door. Frump could see quite plainly that the Sheriff had a firm grip on Frankie's left ear, but she chose to ignore that. "Why, Sheriff Snodgrass," she said brightly, "how lovely of you to drop by. Come on in the kitchen. I've just taken a fresh apple cobbler out of the oven."

Sheriff Snodgrass followed Frump toward the kitchen, still holding onto Frankie. "But first, there's business, Miz Frump. Serious business."

"Oh dear," Frump sighed, finally forced to confront the situation.

"Old Man Gulley has been complaining about his cows' milk turning sour," said the Sheriff. "I have investigated, Miz Frump, and I have found the culprit."

"They've been eating bitterweed," Frump said hopefully.

"No, Miz Frump, *this* culprit." He gave Frankie's ear a shake, and Frankie yelped. "I caught young Frankie riding those cows."

"Oh dear," Frump said. "Frankie, is that so?"

"At a gallop, Miz Frump," said the Sheriff. "Cows ain't meant to be ridden, Miz Frump, especially at a gallop."

Just at that moment, the entire band of Hooligans burst into the room and dashed about, yelling and war-whooping—Eugene in the lead, holding a freshly-caught catfish, the others trying

mightily to catch him. They boiled around the room in a tornado of noise and motion. "Children! Now, children!" Frump called out, reaching this way and that, but grabbing nothing but air. Sheriff Snodgrass could only look on with horror. With a sudden jerk, Frankie broke free from the Sheriff's grasp and scampered out the door, laughing joyously, as if he had just discovered a chunk of beef brisket in his stir fry, the other children following in his wake. Sheriff Snodgrass made a half-hearted attempt to grab Frankie, then gave up and collapsed into a chair. "Mrs. Frump, that boy, that boy. . . " he made a weak gesture in Frankie's direction.

"He is an energetic and ingenious young man, Sheriff Snodgrass. Why, Frankie was telling me the other day that he aspires to be a law enforcement officer just like yourself—a champion of truth and justice."

"Miz Frump," said the Sheriff wearily, "you can't be a law enforcement officer if you have a criminal record. And I'd say that's where that energetic and ingenious young man is headed."

"Now, Sheriff," Frump said, "it can't be as grim as all that."

"And he's not the only one," the Sheriff exclaimed. (He, too was given to exclamations, especially where the Hooligans were involved.) "I'm out here constantly—neighbors calling about your young'uns chasing each other up and down the road with garden implements, putting bedsheets on their heads and scaring poor old widow ladies. Miz Frump, you have a problem with discipline."

Frump gave Sheriff Snodgrass a long, quizzical look while she thought of what she should say. And then she brightened considerably. "Sheriff, these are fine young people. We've just got to find ways to channel their boundless energy into constructive avenues. We've got to emphasize socialization, fraternalization, and matriculation."

"Huh?" said Sheriff Snodgrass with a quizzical look of his own, which he often did when confronted with words of more than four syllables.

"And you can bet we will," Frump continued, "starting right away. You and the other members of the Board of Trustees will see improvement, Sheriff Snodgrass. Improvement!"

And with that, Sheriff Snodgrass rose quickly from his chair and backed out the door and didn't stop until he reached his Sheriff's Department cruiser and headed back toward town. As usual, he was thoroughly buffaloed by Frump, who had such a cheerful attitude toward the thorniest of problems that she seemed to make a molehill out of just about any mountain.

Sheriff Snodgrass was the chairman of the orphanage Board of Trustees, and the members included several prominent local citizens—the school superintendent, the chairman of the county commission, and the minister of the Baptist Church. But ask anyone in the community who really ran the Board of Trustees, and they would tell you it was Ethel, Myrtle and Hortense—three ladies who were known far and wide as the Busybodies. They were very prim and proper ladies with very definite ideas about how other people should act and with plenty of time on their hands to meddle in everyone else's business. They were the kind of ladies who finished their Christmas shopping by the first of July, kept their own homes spic and span, and made sure their husbands got weekly haircuts. They wore mostly brown and gray clothing, tied their hair in buns, and had absolutely no sense of humor. They were easily upset, and what *most* easily upset them was disorganization and rowdiness. As you can imagine, they were kept in a constant state of upsetification by affairs at the orphanage.

The Busybodies were frequent visitors at the orphanage, always barging in unannounced and uninvited at all hours of the day and night, usually at the worst possible moment, notepads in hand, creating havoc with their impromptu inspections.

"Aaaagh! Dust!" Hortense would bellow, passing a white-gloved hand beneath a piece of furniture as Frump followed, swiping ineffectually at the dust with a mop.

"Aaaagh! Cobwebs!" Myrtle would cry, poking about in corners and windowsills as Frump followed, attacking the cobwebs with a feather duster.

"Aaaagh! Cooties!" Ethel would shriek, picking up a well-used handkerchief from the floor as Frump tried unsuccessfully to gather the various pieces of flotsam and jetsam left behind in the wake of eight rambunctious children.

"Chaos and confusion, untidiness and uncleanliness!" they would all chime in together. And invariably, just as they were concluding their inspection and furiously scribbling notes on their notepads, the children would gallop through, yelling and war-whooping, swirling about the Busybodies like a swarm of locusts and utterly ignoring the ladies' cries of disapproval. The Busybodies would retreat in horror, bustling out the door and making a beeline for town to recite all of their grievances to the other members of the Board of Trustees.

Frump knew full well that the Busybodies thought she was getting too old and frazzled to handle the orphanage. She knew full well that they were compiling a long and growing list of criticisms and complaints about her management—or mismanagement—of the rowdy kids and the business of keeping them clean, fed, and mostly out of trouble. Every time Sheriff Snodgrass had to make a trip to the orphanage to handle a complaint, every time the school reported a fracas involving one of the kids, the list grew longer and longer. Frump could put two and two together, and she knew the Busybodies were conducting a campaign to replace her at Peaceful Valley.

But Frump was as fierce as a mama lion about her kids, and she knew that, despite what might be her faults and shortcomings, they needed her and she needed them. Over the years she had made the Peaceful Valley Orphanage a warm and caring place. Children arrived from time to time feeling frightened and lonely and in need of a refuge. Frump couldn't erase the hurtful things that might have happened to them in the past, but she could—and did—give them a home where they felt safe. And she could—and did—love them even when they aggravated the Dickens out of her. The orphanage was Frump's life. She just couldn't imagine doing anything else.

But the Busybodies could.

3 ✻ The Traveling Troubadour

There was, in the same general area and at about the same time, a young man who called himself the Traveling Troubadour. He was a tall and lanky fellow with a mop of unruly hair, a ready smile, and a lovely singing voice. He was both a writer and singer of songs, and the songs he wrote had catchy lyrics and sprightly melodies. Folks came from miles around to hear him when he appeared at various local concerts and talent contests. Though he called himself the Traveling Troubadour, in truth he had never traveled much beyond Knob Hill, where he was born and raised. Folks were always saying, "Go seek your fame and fortune! Let the rest of the world discover your charm and talent!" Folks said it so frequently, and with such conviction, that the Traveling Troubadour decided that he should, indeed, travel.

The only problem was his girlfriend, a dear young lady named Darlene who lived on the other side of Knob Hill. The Troubadour was devoted to Darlene, and she to him. She admired his charm and talent, and thought his mop of unruly hair and ready smile made him quite precious. But she did not share other folks' conviction that he should seek fame and fortune in the wider world. Darlene, quite simply, wanted him all to herself. They had been steady sweethearts since the third grade, and now that they had both graduated from high school, she quite naturally assumed that they would marry and settle down there on Knob Hill, just as her parents and grandparents and great-grandparents had done. It was a good life, she thought, and should be quite enough to satisfy any young man.

But the Troubadour had his dreams. One evening, after winning first prize in a local talent contest, he was walking home with his guitar case in hand when he heard the cry of a night bird from the woods nearby. "Why," he thought to himself, "that bird is as free as the wind, and he can fly and sing anywhere he wants." And it came to him then and there that he, too, must be as free as the wind, and must fly away to try his hand at show business.

Early the next morning he packed a suitcase and a bag lunch of bologna sandwich and banana, took up his guitar case, and trudged down the road to Darlene's house to tell her about his decision. Darlene was, to use a phrase common among Knob Hill folks, fit to be tied.

"Aw, honey-bunch, don't be like that," the Troubadour pleaded.

"Don't call me honey-bunch," she said, stamping her foot. "If I was your honey-bunch, you'd stay here with me instead of going off on a wild toot."

"It's not a wild toot," he protested. I've got music in my soul and rhythm in my fingers. I'm writing all these songs, and people say they're pretty good."

"Then sit here on the porch and pick and sing and write to your heart's content. Sing your songs to me. Sing 'em to Mama and Daddy. They like to have a little music when they're shelling butterbeans."

"But I've gotta see if anybody else thinks my songs are good. And the only place I'm gonna be able to do that is out on the road."

"The road," Darlene snorted. "I've heard what happens to you show-business types out on the road. If you're rotten, nobody will give you the time of day. If you're good, you'll have all sorts of loose women making eyes at you."

"Aw, honey-bunch," he said with a grin. "I'm not interested in any woman but you."

"Then stay here and prove it. I want a man who's reliable. A man who'll settle down and get a steady job and raise a good family. There's all sorts of opportunities right here for a man who'll work hard and keep his priorities straight. Why, Papa was telling me just last night, they're hiring down at the sawmill. You could start tomorrow."

The Troubadour stared at his feet for a moment and ran a hand through his unruly mop of hair. Then he looked up and said, "I gotta try this. Just for a few months. If it doesn't work out, I'll come home and go to work at the sawmill. I've got the rest of my life to settle down. I love you, Darlene. Promise you'll wait for me."

Darlene gave him a hard stare. "I love you, too. But I've got other prospects, and I'm not making any promises."

And with that, she turned on her heel and marched into the house, closing the door rather forcefully behind her. The Troubadour stood there for a moment, torn between love and destiny. Twice, he raised his hand to knock on the door and tell Darlene that he was staying. But twice, he thought to himself, *If I don't do this now, I'll always wish I had.* And that wouldn't be fair to Darlene, either.

So the Troubadour squared his shoulders, picked up his guitar and suitcase and bag lunch, and set off down the road to the intersection where he figured he could thumb a ride to someplace bigger than Knob Hill, someplace where folks might want to hear some catchy new songs from a fellow with music in his soul and rhythm in his fingers.

Would Darlene wait? Would she marry a fellow who already had a job at the sawmill? Would she take a home correspondence course in cosmetology and move off to the city to do cuts and perms? Only time would tell. It was just a chance the Traveling Troubadour would have to take.

So the Troubadour set off to seek his fame and fortune, as many a young person has done over the years.

First of all, he found plenty of good folks willing to give a traveling man a ride—a fellow driving a big eighteen-wheel tractor-trailer full of refrigerated farm produce; a woman at the wheel of a day-care van, who was delighted when the Troubadour pulled out his guitar and entertained the restless kids with catchy songs about frogs and lightning bugs and one-eyed cars and imaginary places where kids made the rules and jellybeans were free. He spent an entire day in the company of a traveling salesman who stopped at every roadside grocery store to hawk his wares of patent medicines and sewing notions. The Troubadour made up a song about one of the salesman's wares, an elixir called Doobey's Nostrum, which was purported to cure ills ranging from hangnails to dyspepsia. The salesman paid the Troubadour five dollars to record the song on a portable tape recorder, and promised that he would play it at all his sales calls.

Finally, the Troubadour alighted from the cab of a pick-up truck, his latest ride, on the corner of a fair-sized town a good way from where he had started. He spotted a coffee shop nearby, where a sign in the window advertised live music every Friday night. It was only Tuesday, but he marched in anyway, pronounced himself available, played and sang a few songs by way of audition, and was hired by the manager for the coming Friday night's performance. Twenty dollars and free coffee, the manager offered. It wasn't much, the Troubadour thought, but it was his first paying job out on the road, and he was proud to get the work and begin the long process of establishing himself as one of America's finest composers and singers of catchy songs.

As he lay himself down to rest that night in a cheap boardinghouse down the street from the coffee shop, he thought to himself, "Well, here goes."

And he slept like a baby.

4 ✳ Christmas Approaches

In the area around Peaceful Valley and Knob Hill, and in the town nearby, there was no more anticipated or relished time of year than Christmas. The town was decorated with colored lights and garland strung from every utility pole, and store windows were coated with spray-on frosting and chock-full of goodies that might tickle gift-giving imaginations.

One reason that the Christmas season always got folks excited was the delicious promise of snow. Right on schedule, a couple of days before Christmas the skies would cloud darkly, the wind would pick up, and the temperature would drop precipitously. Kids would get that sparkle in their eyes and that rosy glow in their cheeks that could only mean snow was on the way. Everybody would get excited—buying up all the milk and bread at the grocery stores, waxing the runners on the sleds, putting out extra seed for the birds. Young and old would stand around with their arms raised, silently praying, "Do it, Lord! Do it!"

But then, nothing would happen. The oldest man in town, so old that he could remember the time he heard President Warren Harding speak on the radio, could not ever remember a Christmas when it snowed. "Oh," he said to one and all who would listen, "it's always looked like snow. Every year, without exception, it's looked like snow. But there's never been a dad-burned flake!"

Now February, that was different. There would always be snow in February, and people would gripe and grouse about the February snow, during which cars slid off the road and kids tracked through their houses with muddy galoshes. "Why not Christmas?" they would cry.

No one knew why, but they didn't let the absence of snow spoil the other delights of the Christmas season. And that was especially true at the Peaceful Valley Orphanage.

It was Frump's favorite time of the year. She became a child again at Christmas—one those fortunate people who, even as an adult, imagined that she heard reindeer on the roof, who loved to fill the house with greenery and good smells and music and wishes. She believed that one thing her orphans needed more than anything was some magic in their lives. And what could be more magical than Christmas?

Each year, she would send Thomas to the woods for a small tree, and when he had it set up in the parlor, she would gather everybody for a decorating party. They would make garlands of popcorn strings, hang hand-made ornaments on the branches, and place a tinfoil star on the very top. Frump and the kids would sing Christmas carols and tell tales of Christmas past and toast each others' good health with hot apple cider.

On Christmas morning there were always plenty of gifts. Folks in the nearby town made sure of that. It was the one time in the year that the orphanage had just about everything it needed. There were bicycles and dolls, cap guns and tea sets. But what the kids treasured most of all were the small, carefully-chosen presents from Frump herself. For Clara, who was steady and serious-minded, there might be a book of wise quotations. For Hilda, who was more romantically inclined, perhaps a record album of love songs. Jenny, who had artistic aspirations, might be favored with a set of watercolor paints. For Eugene, who liked nothing better than leaping and jumping, a pogo stick. For Louann, who could never seem to keep her hands warm, a pair of mittens knitted by Frump herself. Thomas might get a set of wrenches or screwdrivers to help with his various mechanical projects. Frankie, who enjoyed music (especially loud music) when he wasn't riding cows, might get a harmonica. And for Donald, there would perhaps be a box of plant fertilizer for his cherished geranium.

In other words, each gift was special, thought-over long and hard for many months by

Frump, who considered each of her orphans special and unique and worthy of a gift that perfectly fit his or her personality.

As the Christmas of our story approached, with the nights turning frosty and chimney smoke drifting across Peaceful Valley, Frump was in her kitchen preparing a big pot of stir fry one evening when she began to reminisce about the Christmases of her childhood. Frump had come from a large and warm-spirited family who thought of Christmas as both a solemn observance and a time of love and rejoicing. The house was full of aromas—an uncle who smoked a pipe, a grandmother who smelled of lilac water, and a kitchen brimming over with gingerbread cookies and fudge and candied apples. She remembered her father humming "Adeste Fidelis" in his off-key way as he strung colored lights along the eaves of the front porch. And she recalled the evenings when all of the children—brothers and sisters and cousins—would pile into the back of an old truck filled with hay, all of them burrowed deep in blankets and toboggans, and go to see the Living Manger Scene at the church down the road. One year, she had even played the part of a shivering angel, gathered with the wise men and the shepherd boy and Mary and Joseph around the rough-hewn manger where the Baby Jesus (a doll contributed by Frump's sister, Lois) lay.

The memories came back to Frump with such a powerful surge of warm delight, as she stood there over the pot of stir fry, that it made her shiver and giggle.

Then she thought, "Every child should have a Christmas like that."

And then she thought, "But what about my orphans?"

Frump did all she could to make Christmas special and meaningful—a tree, some presents, the joy of giving, the spirit of goodwill.

But families? Real families? No, that was something orphans didn't have and something she couldn't provide.

Or could she?

5 ✶ The Plot

For several days, Frump's mind boiled and bubbled like a pot of stir fry. She considered one idea after another, discarding this detail and adding that, until she had come up with a plan that sent chills of pleasure up her spine and made her ample cheeks even rosier than usual. Why, she could hardly sleep at night for the tumult that her brain was in, and she often arose at small hours of the morning to jot down this note or that to herself.

She revised and re-revised the plan, taking care to work out the details when the children were away at school during the day. She was bursting to tell the orphans, but she wanted to make sure that it was perfect in every way before she spilled the beans. Finally, it was done.

She called the Hooligans together one evening a couple of weeks before Christmas, and when they were all gathered around her, faces bright with expectation, she said, "Children, I've had a fit of inspiration."

"You mean you've been sweating a lot?" asked Louann, whose vocabulary was still forming.

"No, silly, that's *per*spiration," said Jenny, who knew lots of words and had won the fourth-grade spelling bee the year before.

"That's right," said Frump. "Inspiration, not perspiration. Guess what I've found?"

There was a moment of silence as the kids all looked at each other. "The pumpkin Frankie stole from Old Man Gulley's front porch on Halloween?" Eugene volunteered, to which Frankie stuck out his tongue.

Frump shook her head.

"Eugene's other brown sock?" Clara guessed.

"Eugene's other green sock?" Hilda chimed in.

"No," said Frump, looking around at their upturned faces, then taking a deep breath. "A bus."

Every upturned face had a look of serious bafflement.

"And what do you do on a bus?" Frump asked.

"You go to Disney World!" said Louann.

"Well, not that far." Frump smiled. "Christmas will be here before we know it, and this year, I want the holiday to be extra-special. So, on the day before Christmas, we'll get on the bus and take you to homes throughout the county. Some very nice people will have a place set for you at the table, and presents under the tree, and everything. I've matched each and every one of you with a family that I think will be just perfect. A real family!"

The was a dead silence as Frump beamed at them, looking as if she had just won the lottery, or at least a free loaf of bread at the supermarket.

Finally Thomas said, "Well, gee, Frump . . . that sounds like, ah . . . " he looked around at the others for help.

"Fun?" Frankie asked weakly.

"A real riot," Hilda added.

"Yeah," said Jenny, "it gives me goose bumps just thinking about it."

Nobody else said a word.

Frump clapped her hands with glee. "I just knew you'd be pleased!" she cried, and headed off to the kitchen to make another batch of stir fry, her heart full to bursting with the delight of her clever plan that she was sure would bring bounteous joy to the lives of her orphans.

It hadn't been an easy thing for Frump to pull off. There was first the difficulty of securing a bus, and then the matter of finding enough families. She had made a lot of telephone calls all over the county just to line up a handful of families willing to take a Hooligan for a couple of days. But she kept trying, kept appealing to folks' sense of decency and their holiday spirit, and finally came up with a home for each and every one.

Strangely enough, it was not bounteous joy that settled over the Peaceful Valley Orphanage in the days after Frump's blockbuster announcement, but rather a combination of gloom and lethargy. The children moped about when they weren't in school, moving as if they were wading through vats of molasses. Their faces were long and they were given to great, long sighs. Hilda spilled Eugene's chocolate milk on the radio and fried its electronics, so there wasn't even any seasonal music in the house. Mostly, there was just silence.

Frump was so wrapped up in her Christmas plans and the joy of the season that she at first didn't give much notice to the solemn atmosphere. Neither did Thomas, who was normally a quite perceptive young man. Little around the orphanage escaped his attention. But he had been terribly busy with his project for the school science fair, so he had taken scant notice of the state of affairs.

But it eventually dawned on Frump that things weren't quite right, and she remarked upon it one evening three days before Christmas as Thomas struggled in the kitchen door with a load of firewood.

"Gee, it's getting cold out there," Thomas said.

"And looking like snow," said Frump, peering out the kitchen window as she tended supper on the stove.

"Yeah, but you know what that'll amount to," Thomas said. "Like that old fellow in town says, 'Not a dad-burned flake.'"

Thomas stacked the firewood next to the door and then peered over Frump's shoulder. "I see we're having stir fry again."

"The children seem to love it so. And on our limited budget, you can make a little go a long way with stir fry."

"You're the only person I know who makes it by the gallon," Thomas smiled.

Frump stared into the pot for a moment, stirring slowly and thoughtfully, before she said, "Thomas, have you noticed anything different?"

"You've got a new apron?" Thomas guessed.

"No. About the children."

"What about 'em?"

Frump set her spoon down on the counter and turned to Thomas, hands on hips. "We haven't had a bloody nose or broken lamp for days. Eugene hasn't jumped off the roof, Frankie hasn't ridden a single cow, and Hilda hasn't tried to wear even the least little smidgen of make-up. There hasn't been even one call from the school about misbehavior. And Sheriff Snodgrass hasn't been out here all week. It's quiet. *Too* quiet. What's going on, Thomas?"

"Gee, Frump, nothing I know about," said Thomas, scratching his head.

"It doesn't have anything to do with the bus, does it?"

"I don't think so," Thomas said carefully. "I think the bus is a great idea." Then he paused, cocked his head, and gave Frump a searching look. "Have you told Sheriff Snodgrass and the other Trustees what you're doing? The bus and the families and all?"

"Oh," said Frump breezily, "I'll take care of that."

"It's only a couple of days away," he said. "I don't want you to get in any trouble."

"Trouble?" Frump exclaimed, "why the words 'trouble' and 'Christmas' don't belong in the same sentence. I want this to happen more than anything in the world, Thomas. If I can make this Christmas special for all of you, one you'll always remember, it will be the crowning achievement of my years at the orphanage."

Thomas saw how bright and excited her eyes were, how she fairly glowed with goodness and holiday spirit. So he gave her a great hug and said, "Don't worry. It'll be special. I'm sure of it."

6 ✹ The Meeting

Sure enough, just as Frump had said, there was clearly something going on. Thomas observed that the rest of the orphans were moping about the house with long faces, rarely raising their voices, playing quietly when they played at all, and—a sure sign of trouble—even occasionally taking naps. There were no mad gallops through the house, no war whoops. The school holidays had begun, and the orphanage should have been a place of unbridled excitement and joyous anticipation. Instead, it was like a helium balloon which had lost all its helium. Thomas made his annual trip to the woods and brought back a nice little spruce tree and set it up in the parlor. And he and Frump and the other kids spent an evening decorating. But there didn't seem to be much spirit to it, even when Frump served hot apple cider and chocolate chip cookies.

The more Thomas thought about it, the more he began to suspect what might be amiss. As Frump's trusted right-hand man, he knew that it was up to him to find out for sure, and to do something about it. So he did what any good right-hand man would do: he called a meeting the next afternoon.

He started off by trying to inject a light-hearted note. "Hey, guys, I've got a surprise. Guess what we're having for dinner tonight."

"What day is it?" Frankie asked.

"Wednesday," Clara answered.

"Then it's stir fry," Frankie said.

Donald chimed in: "We have stir fry four nights a week."

"And most other nights," Hilda said gloomily, "we have stew, with all of Frump's leftovers."

"Including the leftover stir fry," Eugene added.

"Well," said Thomas cheerfully, "what if I told you we're having steak and potatoes tonight?"

"We wouldn't believe you," Jenny said.

"Are we having steak and potatoes?" Louann asked hopefully.

"No," Thomas admitted, "it's stir fry. But I bet we'll have some great meals with the families we're visiting for Christmas. Turkey and dressing and steak and potatoes. I bet we'll roast marshmallows in the fireplace and have hot chocolate and all the candy we can eat—homemade fudge and stuff. It's all pretty exciting, don't you think?"

Thomas looked hopefully around the group. He was met with only frowns and utter silence. "Okay," he said, "let's have it."

The orphans looked at each other, each waiting for one of the others to speak up. Finally, Frankie said, "You've lived here all your life, haven't you Thomas?"

"Since I was a baby."

"So you've never had to go anyplace new."

"I started school, just like you."

"But you never had to go *live* anyplace new."

"Well, no . . ."

"We all have," Clara spoke up as the other kids nodded in agreement. "Most of us had been in a bunch of foster homes before we got here."

"Four," Eugene said, raising his hand.

"Five," Hilda reported.

"Just two," Louann said, "but one of 'em was weird."

Frankie said, "One family I was with—they were nice, but they had some kinda bugs in the house. I didn't stop itching for a month after I left."

"One of mine kept a pet goat in the kitchen," Clara added.

Eugene spoke up. "Sometimes the other kids call you a sissy if you cry."

"Or," said Louann, "the parents get all bent out of shape if you wet the bed."

"I got passed around to uncles and aunts," Donald chimed in. "The last one wanted to plant my geranium," he said, hugging the pot fiercely. "I started screaming and yelling, and they sent me here."

"I felt like a ping-pong ball," Hilda said. "Every time I'd get settled somewhere and get to know a new family, the lady from the Social Services Department would come get me and take me somewhere else."

"It's not easy starting over, always being the new kid," Clara said.

"Or the smallest," said Louann the munchkin.

"People looking at you like you just flew in from Mars and you've got antennas instead of ears," Eugene said.

Frankie said, "They try to make you feel at home, and ask you what your favorite food is, and give you your own drawer to put your clothes in. . . "

"I always just kept my clothes in my suitcase," said Clara, "because I knew I'd be going before long."

"No matter how hard they try," Jenny said, "you know you don't belong."

"But here," Frankie said, "we *do* belong. This is where we want to be. With you and Frump and each other. We're a family."

Thomas nodded thoughtfully. "You're talking about Christmas. And the bus. And the families."

"Yes!" they all agreed.

Well, Thomas thought to himself, *what to do?* The only thing he could think of on the spot was that he needed to think. So he adjourned the meeting and bundled himself in his jacket and toboggan and gloves and went for a long walk down the road from the orphanage, and

through Old Man Gulley's pasture and into the woods beyond, thinking all the while. Finally, he came to a clearing in the woods and sat down on an old stump and arranged his thoughts in front of him so he could take a good look at them.

For Thomas's sake, the Peaceful Valley Orphanage was the only home he had ever known. He just couldn't imagine being anywhere else. And he could see how the others might feel about it, too. Kids might come and go, but there was always a house full, and they were all in the same boat. They might squabble and sometimes even come to blows, but they stuck up for each other and wiped each other's noses and made sure the younger kids wore their galoshes when it rained. They were a house full of people who might have been strangers in other circumstances, but there together they were like brothers and sisters and cousins. The orphanage was home, and they were a family. And families were supposed to be together at Christmas, weren't they?

But then he thought, *who's the one person who's made it that way?* Frump, of course. She was the one constant in all their lives. No matter how bad things might have been in the past, each orphan knew that here with Frump, it would be much better. If you were sad or worried, Frump was the one person in the world you felt completely comfortable talking to. Sometimes she would just listen, and that might be the best thing of all. Other times, she might offer a word of sympathy or even a tidbit of advice. Somehow, Frump could see right down into the middle of your heart, and she knew what kind of things in your heart made it special and different from any other. Thomas was sure that if you looked up the word "love" in the dictionary, Frump's picture would be right beside the definition. Or at least, it should be.

Thomas thought about all this for a good while as the afternoon settled about him and the cold nipped at his nose and the wind sighed through the trees. Old Man Gulley's cows lowed from the nearby pasture as they headed for the barn and warm hay. Finally, with his thoughts all sorted out, he rose and went home.

That evening after supper, Thomas called another meeting.

"I've thought about what you said," Thomas told them. "And you're right. You guys are my family, and this is home. But here's something else I want you to think about: Frump has gone to an awful lot of trouble to line up the bus and the families and all that. She wants more than anything in the world for us to have a special Christmas. It's a present she's giving us. So what can we give Frump? We can go and enjoy ourselves, and when it's done, give Frump a big hug and tell her how much we appreciate her. It would be a big, special present." He paused and looked around the circle of faces. "We love Frump, don't we?"

"Of course," they all said emphatically.

"Sometimes, you do something for somebody, even though it may not be what you really *want* to do, even though it might even be hard, because you love 'em. So can we do this for Frump?"

The kids all looked at each other. After a moment, it was Clara who spoke up. "Yes, Thomas. Of course we can."

The others nodded.

"Be on our best behavior?" Thomas went on. And with a look at Frankie, "No cow riding?"

Frankie grinned. "I'll try."

"Good," Thomas said with a sigh of relief. "And who knows, it may even turn out to be a real adventure."

7 ✳ The Troubadour Revisited

nd then there was the Traveling Troubadour.

By this time, shortly before Christmas, he had been out on the road for several months, seeking fame and fortune. He had found absolutely none of either.

First of all, it was hard to find places to perform. He went from night club to coffee house, from senior citizen center to elementary school, from church social hall to fast food restaurant, asking for a chance to display his talent.

"But we've never heard of you before," people would say.

"Of course not," the Troubadour would reply. "I'm just getting started. May I audition for you?"

Often, they would let him sing a couple of his songs. "Catchy and clever," they would say, "but we've never heard them before."

"Of course not," the Troubadour would reply. "I just wrote them."

Occasionally, he would be hired to perform—perhaps in a coffee shop or a roadhouse out on some lonesome highway. The jobs never paid very much money, so the Troubadour supplemented his income by washing dishes, sweeping floors, washing cars, digging ditches—anything he could find to stretch the meager earnings from his musical performances. After all, a Traveling Troubadour had to have a bite to eat and a place to sleep and a way to get from town to town.

When he did perform, he learned quickly that there were two kinds of audiences: people who listened, and people who didn't. Most didn't. Most people just wanted a little background music while they sipped their coffee or gossiped or exchanged opinions about world affairs. To those audiences, the Troubadour sang his heart out, but he knew that most of what he sang

went right over people's heads and right out the door. Every once in a while, after a performance, someone would step up and say, "Hey, I really like your songs. They are catchy and clever." But not often.

Back in late November, as the weather had been turning nippy and the Troubadour was wishing he could afford a nice, warm jacket, a man stepped up after a performance and introduced himself as the owner of a radio station. "Your songs are catchy and clever," the man said. "Would you like to perform them on my radio station?"

"You betcha," said the Traveling Troubadour.

So the man paid the Troubadour ten dollars to sing a half-hour's worth of songs on a morning radio show. Since the holiday season was approaching, the Troubadour ended the half-hour with a song he had just written the night before, titled "Santa Wears Cowboy Boots." Two people called in to say they thought the songs were catchy and clever, especially the one about Santa and the cowboy boots. The radio man made a recording of the Santa song and said he'd keep playing it through the holiday season. The Troubadour took the ten dollars he earned from his radio performance and bought two doughnuts and a bus ticket to the next town.

As November turned into December, the weather got colder and colder, and the Traveling Troubadour got lonesomer and lonesomer, especially for his girlfriend Darlene. He missed her terribly and wondered what she was doing back there on Knob Hill, or if she was even there at all. In the beginning, after he first hit the road seeking fame and fortune, he tried calling her on the telephone. But her Mama would always say, "Darlene's out, and I don't know when she'll be back." The Troubadour tried writing letters, in which he told Darlene of the big, empty place in his heart where she used to be. The letters all went unanswered. He began to write songs of lost love and heartache, but he knew that nobody wanted to hear such sad stuff, especially right before Christmas. So he kept those all to himself.

And so it happened that the Traveling Troubadour found himself, several days before Christmas, in a grubby little roadhouse in an out-of-the-way town you never heard of, several states and many miles away from Knob Hill. He sat on a stool and strummed his guitar and sang his heart out, putting all his talent and energy into his performance, but he could tell from the get-go that this was not a crowd of listeners. Most of them sat there sipping on sarsaparilla or other beverages and trading gossip and opinions about world affairs. A few seemed to be on the verge of dozing off. And one poor fellow was sleeping peacefully on the floor underneath a table.

The Troubadour finished a rendition of "Santa Wears Cowboy Boots," and waited for a polite moment for applause. Not a single hand clapped. Not a single person was paying the least bit of attention.

Suddenly, quite out of the blue and completely unannounced, the Traveling Troubadour was struck by a vision: in his imagination, he pictured himself at his parents' table back home, with aunts and uncles and cousins, brothers and sisters, gathered around for Christmas dinner. Darlene was at his side, holding his hand under the table while his father said the blessing. There was a gaily-decorated tree in the corner and the scattered remnants of wrapping paper from Christmas morning present-opening. There were the delicious smells of turkey and dressing, green bean casserole and candied yams, hot cider and homemade fudge. And it was then and there that the Traveling Troubadour said to himself, *"It's time to go home."*

So without a moment's hesitation, he climbed down from his stool, packed away his guitar, fetched his suitcase from where he had stashed it behind the stage, marched out the front door, and stood at the edge of the nearby road with his thumb out. After a while, a truck driver stopped and gave him a ride.

8 ✳ The Bus

It was early on the morning of Christmas Eve day. Everyone at the Peaceful Valley Orphanage was sleeping soundly, except for Frump. She had arisen long before daybreak, wrapped herself warmly in scarf, overcoat and boots, and hitched a ride with Old Man Gulley, who was delivering milk from his dairy farm to the nearby town. She returned to Peaceful Valley an hour later, with the sky just beginning to pale in the east, behind the wheel of a wheezing, clanking, groaning bus. It gasped for breath as it labored up each rise in the road, and backfired in weary protest as it descended the downside. Its paint—what there was left of it—was faded and peeling, much like the orphanage itself, and the poor old bus lumbered along on tires that were so bald they could have been used in a commercial for hair growth treatment. If you looked very closely at the sides of the bus, you could barely make out the faded letters: HOOTERVILLE HEADKNOCKERS.

Frump pleaded with the bus to make it up the last rise to the orphanage, and breathed a sigh of relief when it coughed and clattered and finally came to rest in the orphanage yard. She turned off the engine and waited in the silence to make sure no one in the house had heard her approach. And then as dawn broke, she climbed out and started decorating. She hummed Christmas carols to herself as she draped the sides of the bus in red and green bunting, tucked sprigs of greenery around the bumpers and in the spots along the sides of the bus where the frame had rusted through, and then hung a huge hollyberry wreath on the radiator. Finally, she stepped back and admired her handiwork with glee, clapping her hands and singing a couple of bars from Handel's "Messiah." *Hallelujah!* Just then, she was startled by a voice behind her that said, "Holy Moley, Frump? What is *that thing*?"

34

She turned to see Thomas standing there, shivering in pajamas and bathrobe, hair tousled and eyes puffy from sleep. "Why," she said, "any ninny can see it's a Christmas Bus!"

Thomas just stared. Then he stared some more. And then he began a slow journey around the bus, staring and shaking his head and quite forgetting how cold he was. Finally, he arrived again at the front of the bus. He gave the bus one more mournful look and said, "That's it?"

Frump beamed. "How do you like my decorations? Doesn't it look festive!"

"Where did you get it?"

"I borrowed it."

"From a junkyard?"

"No, silly. From the Hooterville Headknockers."

"The baseball team?"

"Yes."

"Golly, Frump, that old bucket of bolts has broken down on just about every highway in this part of the state. Most times you see it on the road, it's being towed."

"Well, Mister Mechanical Wizard," Frump said, "it's your job to keep it running."

"Me?"

"Of course. How do you think you'll ever win the Nobel Prize for Thing-A-Ma-Jigs if you can't handle something as simple as a bus."

Thomas just shook his head again.

"Now go get some clothes on and let's get organized before the children wake up," she said. "There's a lot to do, and I can't do it without my trusty right-hand man."

Thomas was back shortly, dressed and bundled and carrying a box of tools. He poked around the engine for a bit, made a few minor adjustments, then had Frump crank the engine while he stuck his head into the engine compartment and listened with a practiced ear.

"Did you fix it?" Frump asked.

"It's a little better, but you're sure gonna have to take it easy with this thing. It could come apart at the seams at any moment."

Frump switched off the engine and climbed out of the bus, carrying a large folded sheet of paper, which she opened to reveal a map, spreading it across the hood of the bus. "Okay, here's where we're going. First," her finger traced the route, "we'll take the back way over to Shady Grove and deliver Clara to the Carver family."

"It would be a lot shorter to go through town," Thomas observed.

"Oh no," Frump said emphatically. "We definitely *don't* want to go through town. I want all of you to enjoy some good, clean country air, the smell of wood fires and pine needles. There's nothing quite like Christmas in the country."

Thomas eyed her suspiciously as she went on. "So Clara to Shady Grove, then we'll take Donald over to the Jones family at Roaring Creek . . . "

As she spoke, something caught Thomas's eye and he looked up from the map and down the hill toward the nearby road. "Frump," he said, "is that the Sheriff's car turning in off the road?"

Frump jumped as if she'd had an electric shock, gathered up the map and thrust it at Thomas. "Quick!" she cried. "Hide the bus!"

"What?"

"Drive it around back of the barn! Out of sight!"

"Frump," Thomas said, his eyes growing wide, "you didn't tell 'em, did you?"

"No questions, Thomas. Just do it!"

So Thomas scrambled into the bus, fired it up, threw it into reverse, and started backing away. Sheriff Snodgrass always parked his cruiser at the bottom of the hill, rather than drive up the driveway to the orphanage building. The driveway was full of ruts and potholes and mud puddles, and the Sheriff was leery of getting his nice new car muddy or damaged. So he came trudging up a gravel path, as usual, this time carrying two large sacks. Frump stood there watching his slow but steady progress, trying mightily to hide the fact that she was nervous enough to bust buttons from her overcoat. "Sheriff Snodgrass!" she called out merrily as he approached, "Merry Christmas to you!"

"And Merry Christmas to you," he called back as he huffed and puffed up the hill.

"Say," Frump called, "have you put the snow tires on your cruiser? This could be the year. Just look at those clouds up there. Looks an awful lot like snow to me. Maybe you should go back to town and put on those snow tires and come back later. I'll have a fresh apple cobbler by then."

Sheriff Snodgrass finally reached her, bending over to catch his breath for a moment, then wheezing, "Aw, Miz Frump, anybody knows it's not gonna snow around here at Christmas. Always looks like it, but never does. It's a tradition." He held out the two sacks he was carrying. "I brought you folks some turkeys."

Frump took the sacks. "That's mighty nice of you, Sheriff. Now about those snow tires . . ."

Sheriff Snodgrass sniffed the air. "Is that gasoline I smell?"

"Gasoline?" Frump cried in near panic. "Gasoline?"

"And did I hear some kind of engine up here?"

"Engine?" she cried. "Engine?"

At that moment, with Frump feeling faint from anxiety, Thomas appeared from behind the barn. "Engine?" he said. "Probably the well pump starting up. It's making an awful lot of racket these days, Sheriff. I need to do a little work on it."

"What about the gasoline smell? The well pump doesn't run on gasoline."

"Aw," said Thomas, "that's probably coming from the sawmill back over the hill there. I think I heard 'em crank up a bit earlier."

Sheriff Snodgrass gave Frump a long, searching look. "Is everything all right out here?"

"Couldn't be better," she said brightly.

"Well," said the Sheriff, giving the situation a long look-over, "all right then. I guess I'd better be heading along. I'm doing all the patrolling on my own today. I've given my deputies the day off so they can be with their families and get their last-minute shopping done. Not much to patrol about, though. Nothing ever happens the day before Christmas."

"Of course not!" Frump and Thomas said in unison.

Sheriff Snodgrass turned to go, waving over his shoulder. "Bye now. Merry Christmas."

"Merry Christmas!" they called out as he went back down the hill, scarcely daring to breathe until the Sheriff had climbed into his cruiser, started the engine, and pulled away.

And then Thomas turned to Frump and gave her a wry look. "Frump . . ."

"Yes?" she said innocently.

"Why didn't you tell the Trustees?"

"They don't have any imagination," she said fiercely. "At least, those Busybodies don't. All they know how to say is 'no.' And they would have said 'no' about all this because they can't see past the ends of their noses."

"And what are we going to do if you . . . if we . . . get caught?"

"We'll think of something, Thomas. We're going to make this work. It has to. It's Christmas, and good things happen at Christmas. Have faith, Thomas. Just have faith. And be creative!"

9 ✳ On The Road

In short order, Frump and Thomas had the Hooligans up, dressed, and on the road. With Sheriff Snodgrass out patrolling early this Christmas Eve morning, Frump was taking no chances of getting caught and having her carefully-laid plans spoiled. She wasn't so much worried about the Sheriff himself as she was his fellow members of the Board of Trustees, the Busybodies. Once she had the children delivered to their Christmas families, she didn't mind what the Busybodies might do to her. But she would move heaven and earth to keep them from spoiling what she knew would be the children's best Christmas ever.

It was still quite early, and the children had been rousted grumpily from their beds. So as the bus rumbled along, they did what sleepy children always do when their naps have been interrupted—they went back to sleep, slumping against each other on the stiff vinyl seats, swaying to and fro as the bus rocked from side to side.

Thomas sat alone in the very front seat, right behind Frump, watching as she steered the bus along the back roads.

"So far so good," Frump chirped happily. "The bus is running just fine, Thomas."

"It sounds like it's got whooping cough," he said, as he listened to the wheezing and coughing of the ancient engine.

"Nonsense. Check the map and let's see about our first stop."

"Where is the map?" Thomas asked, looking around.

"I thought you had it."

"I thought *you* had it."

"Oh well," Frump said, "it doesn't matter. I know where we're going."

They wheezed along for another mile or so before something occurred to Thomas. "Frump, I didn't see your name on the map. Which family will you be with for Christmas?"

"Oh, I'll be fine. I'll pop some popcorn and make a fresh, new apple cobbler. Then I'll get up in the morning and feed the birds and then maybe spend the day cleaning up."

"At the orphanage? By yourself?"

"It'll be nice having the place empty for a day," she said hopefully. "I'll get a lot done."

"Frump!" Thomas protested, "that's terrible!"

"Now, don't you go worrying about me," Frump reassured him. "I'll be just fine. This is *your* holiday. Just knowing that you're all with real families—why, that's the best Christmas present I could possibly have."

Thomas shook his head. It was just like Frump to think of everybody but herself. She was the most unselfish person he knew, and he hoped that when he became a famous mechanical engineer, he would be the same way—kind, considerate, always thinking of others before himself. But still, he was powerfully troubled by the thought of Frump spending Christmas Day by herself at the orphanage, with all her beloved kids enjoying themselves somewhere else. But what to do? The plans were made, the project set in motion. Thomas wracked his brain, trying to think of something.

But as he was wracking with great mental exertion, Frump suddenly cried out, "Oh my goodness!"

Thomas roused himself. "What?"

Frump was peering intently at the rear-view mirror, eyes wide. "Oh, my dear, dear goodness!"

Thomas turned to look out the rear window of the bus, over the heads of the sleeping children, and well back in the distance, he could see the flashing red and blue lights of . . . Sheriff Snodgrass's cruiser! And then he heard the faint sound of the cruiser's siren, getting louder by the second.

Frump stomped on the gas pedal. The engine howled in protest, but it slowly responded and the bus began to pick up speed. The faster it went, the more it wheezed and coughed and backfired and rocked from side to side. Frump gripped the steering wheel so hard that Thomas was afraid she might break it right off.

The Hooligans began to wake up. "Hey," Eugene cried, "what's going on?"

"Frump, what's happening?" Clara yelled.

"Frump's driving like a maniac!" said Donald.

"Yeah!" the kids all shouted.

"Thomas said we might have an adventure," said Hilda.

"But this is better than the circus!"

"Or a food fight!"

"Better than riding a cow!" Frankie yelped with glee.

Thomas turned to look back at the kids, who had quite obviously decided that this was all great fun. "Hang on, everybody!" he commanded. "Frump," he said, turning back to her, "you can't outrun him. The jig's up!"

Frump's mouth was set in a grim line. "Oh, no it's not." And just then she spotted another road bearing off to the right, a narrow dirt road with thick woods on either side. "We'll turn right here!" She gave the steering wheel a vigorous turn and the bus careened around the corner, the kids hanging onto each other for dear life as the bus rocked almost up onto two wheels and then, to Frump's great relief, made the turn and barreled down the side road.

10 ✳ An Impromptu Field Trip

At that very moment, who should be standing at the roadside—wearing an old overcoat and a slouch hat, sitting on his guitar case, flapping his arms in a vain attempt to stay warm, looking thoroughly miserable—but the Traveling Troubadour. He had been on the road for several days, hitching rides, trying to get home to Darlene for Christmas. He was nearly there, but the last fellow he rode with had dropped him off an hour before. By now he was chilled to the bone, hoping some Good Samaritan would come along and give him a lift the final couple of miles to Knob Hill.

The Christmas Bus was not quite what he had in mind. It bore down on the Troubadour, rattling and quivering and making all manner of horrible noises, as if it might come completely apart at any moment, leaving only a jumble of bolts and a covey of dazed children in the middle of the road. Through the windshield, he could see the wide-eyed, terrified face of poor Frump gripping the steering wheel, and as she suddenly spotted the Troubadour, becoming even more wide-eyed and terrified than ever.

"Good gawdamighty!" the Troubadour bellowed, leaping to his feet, grabbing his suitcase and guitar case and scrambling away from the edge of the road. There was a howl of screeching metal as Frump jammed on the brakes and the bus came to a lurching halt at the place where the Troubadour had been sitting just mere seconds before.

Frump was frozen in place in the driver's seat, her hands gripping the steering wheel, a look of horror on her face. Behind her in the bus, there was pandemonium—the kids laughing and yelling, thinking that this was the most exciting ride they had ever had.

"Frump!" Thomas cried, but she didn't bat an eye. Out in the distance, Thomas could hear

44

the siren of Sheriff Snodgrass's car, drawing closer and closer. Nothing to do but take charge. Thomas turned to the kids. "Everybody out!" he commanded. "Leave your stuff! Quick! Quick!" He herded the kids quickly off the bus, and they milled around in noisy confusion as the Troubadour, still shaky from his near-miss, hustled over.

"Hey, you folks all right? I thought you were gonna plumb run over me."

Thomas gave the Troubadour a quick look-over, then turned to the kids. "Follow him!" he said, pointing at the Troubadour.

"What?" the Troubadour asked, thoroughly confused.

"Into the woods," Thomas said. "Keep 'em quiet! Go!"

Thomas was so convincing that the Troubadour grabbed up his guitar case and suitcase and dashed toward the nearby woods with the kids scrambling behind him, leaving Thomas standing by the bus and Frump still frozen to the steering wheel. The Troubadour and the kids were barely out of sight when Sheriff Snodgrass's car came careening around the corner onto the dirt road and slid to a stop behind the bus. Thomas uttered not a word as the Sheriff turned off the siren and the engine, climbed out of the car, and strode over to the bus, his eyes narrowing as he spotted Frump and Thomas. Frump gave a vigorous shake of her head, came to her senses, and waved delicately through the windshield at the Sheriff. "Good morning, Sheriff Snodgrass," she called out.

The Sheriff stopped in his tracks and took in the scene—the bus, Frump, and Thomas. He stared for a long time before he nodded and said, "Miz Frump . . . Thomas . . ." Then he walked slowly around the bus, examining it carefully, while Frump watched anxiously and Thomas followed, keeping a healthy distance between himself and the Sheriff. When the Sheriff had made a complete circle of the bus, he stepped to the open doorway, peered in at Frump, and said, "You folks want to tell me what's going on here?"

"We're making deliveries," said Frump, not wanting to tell Sheriff Snodgrass either the complete truth or a complete fib.

"That's right," Thomas agreed, "spreading Christmas cheer."

Sheriff Snodgrass took off his hat, scratched his head, and put his hat back on. "In a bus?"

"Well . . . " said Frump, and smiled weakly.

"Where did you get this bus, Miz Frump?"

Frump pondered that for a moment. "I borrowed it," she said firmly.

"Well, you can't drive it."

"I admit, I'm a little rusty behind the wheel . . . " she started to say.

"It doesn't have any brake lights."

Frump's hand went to her mouth. "Oh, dear."

"You'll have to take it back to the orphanage, Miz Frump," the Sheriff said firmly. "I'll follow right behind you. We'll use the brake lights on my cruiser." He turned toward his car. "Just take it real slow."

Frump and Thomas looked at each other—a look that bordered on panic.

"But it won't run, Sheriff," Thomas blurted.

The Sheriff turned back to Thomas and gave him a long, searching look. "What do you mean, it won't run? It was running like a bat out of Hades a minute ago."

"But the engine was acting up something awful," Thomas went on quickly. "That's why we turned down this side road. And then it just quit."

Sheriff Snodgrass gave Thomas a look of powerful suspicion. "Is that so?"

"You betcha," Thomas said, as he stepped quickly to the front of bus, opened the hood, and stuck his head inside the engine compartment. He fumbled around in the tangle of gears, pistons and wires for a moment, then called out to Frump, "Frump, try her now." Frump just gave him a blank look. "The engine, Frump. See if she'll start."

"Oh," Frump said brightly. "Right." She turned the ignition key. The engine groaned and moaned . . . *R-R-R-R-R* . . . but that was all.

Sheriff Snodgrass peered into the innards of the bus's engine.

"Again," Thomas said.

R-R-R-R-R-R . . .

Again, nothing.

"See," Thomas said to the Sheriff, "she won't run."

Frump nodded vigorously. "Won't run!"

The Sheriff stared at Thomas and Frump, then again at the engine. "What do you reckon is wrong with her, Thomas?"

"I'd say," Thomas hesitated, searching for just the right diagnosis, "it's probably an internal combustion problem."

"Good thinking!" said Frump

"Internal combustion," Sheriff Snodgrass said thoughtfully. "Can you fix it?"

"Not here," Thomas said.

"Definitely not here," Frump said emphatically, getting into the spirit of things.

Sheriff Snodgrass took off his hat again, scratched his head, and put his hat back on. "Well, I don't know a dang thing about machinery."

"Good," Thomas said before he caught himself.

"What?"

"I mean," Thomas said quickly, "it's a good thing I do."

"He's a regular mechanical whiz!" Frump cried.

The Sheriff turned toward his cruiser. "I guess I'll have to call Dub's Garage on my radio and get him to come out here and tow her in."

Frump and Thomas exchanged another worried look. "He's not there!" Thomas cried. "Christmas Eve, he's closed. Probably doing his last-minute shopping. You'll have to go track him down, Sheriff."

"Track him down," Frump repeated with another vigorous nod of her head.

Sheriff Snodgrass wrinkled his nose and scrunched up his mouth, which he often did when pondering a dilemma. "All right," he said after a moment, "you two come with me. I'll drop you off at the orphanage, then take care of the bus."

"Oh, we couldn't do that," Frump said. "A borrowed bus? We feel responsible, don't we, Thomas?"

"Responsible," Thomas agreed solemnly. "Mighty responsible. Yessirree, Sheriff. We are responsible for this here bus." He patted the fender of the bus protectively.

Thomas and Frump gave the Sheriff a sweet, innocent smile that played nicely against his perplexed frown. "Miz Frump, who's taking care of those wild Hooligans back at the orphanage?"

Frump had to think about that for a bit. "Oh," she said finally, "they're just fine, Sheriff. They're on. . . they're on a field trip! With a nice young fellow who's watching over them. They're on their best behavior, believe me. So you don't have to worry a bit."

The Sheriff took in the scene one last time—the rickety old bus, grinning Frump and Thomas—then gave a shake of his head, threw up his hands in frustration and started again toward his cruiser.

"Merry Christmas, Sheriff," Frump and Thomas called gaily.

The Sheriff gave them a wave over his shoulder, climbed into his cruiser, started the engine, and pulled away. Frump and Thomas watched until he was out of sight, then both breathed a huge sigh of relief.

"That was a close call," Thomas said.

"Yes, it was." Frump wrung her hands. "But what are we going to do now?"

"Get the heck out of here."

11 ✳ Snoops

Meanwhile, back at the orphanage, who should arrive but the Busybodies: Ethel, Myrtle, and Hortense. What better day to pull a surprise inspection at the orphanage than Christmas Eve, when the children were all out of school, tearing through the house whooping and hollering, leaving all manner of flotsam and jetsam in their wake, with Frump bustling along behind crying, "It's a madhouse!" They would report their findings to the other members of the Board of Trustees and insist that they all visit the orphanage immediately to see first-hand the chaos and confusion. What more evidence would the Trustees need to decide that Frump was indeed too old, too rattled, and too inefficient to continue at the orphanage?

The Busybodies drove to the orphanage in Myrtle's car, yammering all the way about their multitudinous grievances against Frump, and pulled up in the yard at mid-morning. They bustled into the house and set out straightaway to record their findings in their little notebooks.

"Aaaagh! Dust!" Hortense bellowed, wiping her white-gloved hand along a window sill and coming away with several weeks' worth of accumulated grime.

"Aaaagh! Cobwebs!" Myrtle cried, climbing upon a chair to reach a far corner where spiders had long since abandoned their summer habitat.

"Aaaagh! Cooties!" Ethel shrieked, picking up one of Eugene's well-worn socks from the floor beneath his bed.

"Chaos and confusion, untidiness and uncleanliness!" they all shouted in unison. Then they paused for a moment and looked at each other in astonishment.

"Untidiness and uncleanliness to be sure," said Hortense.

"But where is the chaos and confusion?" Myrtle asked.

"It's entirely too quiet," Ethel agreed.

The Busybodies busied themselves from room to room, searching high and low for Hooligans and their Hooligan behavior. But they found not a single, solitary soul. The place was entirely empty.

"What on earth?" Hortense wondered.

"Perhaps they've all run away," Myrtle said. "Conditions got so bad that those poor, dear children just couldn't stand it any more."

"Or . . . she's kidnapped them!" Ethel cried.

"Kidnapped!" they all yelped together, and bustled out the door toward their car, intent on reporting what they were sure must be a dastardly crime to Sheriff Snodgrass, who would no doubt put out an all-points bulletin and have every law enforcement officer in the state on the look-out.

But just as they were about to pile into Myrtle's car, Hortense spotted a piece of paper lying on the ground in the yard. She picked it up, examined it closely, then called out to the others, "Girls, I think I've solved the mystery."

Myrtle and Ethel crowded in close and they all looked at the paper, turning it this way and that. It was, of course, Frump's map—which Thomas had dropped in his haste to hide the bus when the Sheriff arrived unexpectedly earlier that morning.

Now, the Busybodies may have been unforgivably tacky, they may have been horrifyingly conniving, but they were not dumb. When they perused the map, seeing marks at various spots around the county, and the names of all of the orphans connected to the marks, they knew something was afoot, something Frump had obviously cooked up—and worst of all, something that DID NOT HAVE THEIR PERMISSION. Hortense, Myrtle and Ethel looked at the map and looked at each other, and sly smiles spread over their pinched, parsimonious faces.

"Aaaagh!" they all cried. "We've got her now!"

"And," Hortense added, rattling the map with glee, "we know where to find her!"

★ ★ ★

Meanwhile, back at the bus, Frump was wondering how they were going to get the heck out of there. "The bus has a . . . what did you call it, Thomas?"

"An internal combustion problem. Better known as a . . . " he reached into his jacket pocket and withdrew the length of wire he had placed there minutes before while he was rummaging around in the innards of the bus, ". . . a missing spark plug wire."

"Brilliant!" Frump said.

"Well, you said to be creative." Thomas took a few steps toward the nearby woods and called out, "Hey, kids! Time to go!"

There was a rustling about in the underbrush, and after a moment, the orphans emerged, followed by the Traveling Troubadour. Thomas dived once again into the engine of the bus, and replaced the spark plug wire while the kids milled about, talking excitedly.

"Thank you so much," Frump said to the Troubadour. "We really appreciate your help."

"Ma'am," the Troubadour said with a shake of his head, "do you want to tell me what in the Dickens is going on around here?"

The orphans crowded around Frump and the Troubador. "Yeah," Hilda said, "what's up, Frump?"

"Why did you send us to the woods?" Frankie asked.

"What's wrong with the bus?" Clara wanted to know.

"Are we going home now?" Eugene added.

"I'm getting cold," Donald said. "My geranium's getting cold."

"I'm hungry," Louann complained.

Thomas's head emerged from the bus engine and he held up his hands for quiet. "Hey, guys, we're on a secret mission."

"Like in the spy movies?" Jenny asked.

"Exactly," Thomas nodded.

"Are we gonna blow up anything?" That was from Frankie, who thought that blowing up something, as long as it didn't cause any great deal of damage, might be the most delicious kind of mischief you could get into.

"Are we gonna parachute behind enemy lines?" That was from Eugene, who loved to jump from heights, and thought it might be especially fun to do so strapped into a parachute.

Thomas laughed. "It's not that kind of secret mission. This is a stay-quiet-and-out-of-sight kind of secret mission."

Frankie grinned. "I'll bet it's a pull-a-fast-one-on-Sheriff-Snodgrass kind of secret mission." If Frankie couldn't blow up something, he thought that pulling a fast one on his longtime nemesis Sheriff Snodgrass might be almost as delicious.

"That's it," Thomas said. "Let's take a vote. Everybody who wants in. . . "

"Yeah!" the kids cried all at once.

"All right," Thomas ordered. "Everybody on the Christmas bus!"

As the kids scrambled onto the bus, Thomas closed the hood with a satisfied slam. "She's all fixed," he said to Frump. "Even the brake lights."

"Thomas, you're a wizard."

Thomas gave her an aw-shucks grin, then climbed aboard and took his seat just behind

Frump, who turned the ignition key. The bus roared to life. Then she looked out the still-open door of the bus and spied the Traveling Troubadour, standing back a way with his suitcase in one hand and guitar case in the other, looking thoroughly dumbfounded. "Son, are you coming or not?"

"Well . . ."

"You're hitchhiking, aren't you?"

"Yes, ma'am."

"Where are you going?"

"Knob Hill."

"We're going right by there. In fact, it's close to our first stop. We'll drop you off."

"Are you sure it's safe?" the Troubadour asked. "You folks sound like a bunch of desperadoes."

"Frankie rides cows!" Louann yelled, and Frankie stuck out his tongue at her.

"Son," Frump said, "it's Christmas Eve and the day's wasting. There may not be another vehicle by here for hours. You can take your chances with a bunch of desperadoes, or you can stand out here and freeze to death."

The Troubadour considered the alternatives for a fraction of a split second, and then made haste to get aboard.

12 ✳ On To Knob Hill

Frump drove on with a hopeful smile on her face. Up to now, things hadn't gone exactly to plan, and a lesser woman might have just parked the bus and gone home. But Frump was undaunted. She believed that when things got a little tight, something would always turn up. In other words, she believed in serendipity. And she felt a great responsibility to this busload of orphans to make this the most special Christmas of their lives. So she just kept driving, hoping that serendipity would appear around the next curve and help her bring her big project to fruition.

In fact, Frump decided that one very nice bit of serendipity had already turned up in the person of the Traveling Troubadour. By the time the bus had gone a couple of more miles, she had properly introduced him to the orphans and had made him right at home. She explained the situation in detail—the orphanage, the bus, the Busybodies, and the Sheriff. "Yep," said the Troubadour with a grin, "you folks are sure enough a band of desperadoes. Shoot, I might even get a good song out of this little adventure. I'm happy to be along."

The Troubadour was in his element. He was a natural-born showman, never so much at home as he was before an audience—especially, a captive audience. Why, this busload of Hooligans wasn't anything like the coffee shop patrons who prattled and gossiped and did anything *but* pay attention to his music. These kids *listened*. It was, he decided, the best and most appreciative audience he'd had in months.

The Troubadour took his guitar out of its battered old case, tuned it, and started strumming and singing. Frump and the Hooligans joined in, and soon they had a regular hootenanny going. They sang some old familiar tunes—"Bill Grogan's Goat" and "I've Been Working On The Railroad." Then the Troubadour entertained with some of his novelty songs, including one he made up on the spot about a pet geranium that made Donald blush with pleasure. Donald felt very special, having a song written about his dearest possession. In fact, it was the most special he had felt in a great, long while.

"Do you have any Christmas songs in your repertoire?" Frump asked.

"Matter of fact, I sure do." And he told Frump and the kids about "Santa Wears Cowboy Boots," the song he had composed a few weeks back and had sung on the radio.

"Santa wears cowboy boots," he sang. "He wears 'em to deliver his loot. Mrs. Santa Claus says, 'Mighty Cute!' when Santa wears cowboy boots." He sang about how Santa had been staying up late, watching old Western movies on television, when he got the idea of having a Western theme for Christmas. So he had the elves re-tool the toy workshop to turn out six-shooters and chaps and boots and ten-gallon hats. The Troubadour sang the chorus a couple of times, and then had the kids and Frump join in. "Santa wears cowboy boots," they all sang. "He wears 'em to deliver his loot. Mrs. Santa Claus says, 'Might cute!' when Santa wears cowboy boots."

Frump and the kids laughed and applauded when they finished the song. "That's mighty catchy and clever," they all agreed—a song that should be played on the radio along with "Rudolph The Red-Nosed Reindeer" and "Have A Holly, Jolly Christmas."

"Aw, I don't know," said the Troubadour. "To tell you the truth, I haven't had much luck with my songs. I've been out on the road for months, trying to get a start in show business, and you folks are the first people who took time to really listen to my music."

"We think you're pretty talented," Frump said.

"I used to think so, too," said the Troubadour. "But I'm giving it up and heading home."

The Christmas Bus topped a rise and dipped into a shallow valley with another hill on the other side. "Knob Hill's just ahead, Mister Troubadour," Frump said. "Where do you want to get off?"

"Right up there," the Troubadour pointed. "That little white house with the green shutters."

"Home sweet home," said Clara wistfully.

"Well, not mine," the Troubadour said. "It's where my girlfriend lives."

"I bet she'll be glad to see you," said Jenny.

The Troubadour shook his head and opened his guitar case and put the guitar away. "I don't know. When I took off a few months ago, she put up a powerful fuss."

"Then why did you?"

"I just had to give it a try. You never know whether or not you can do something until you try. I tried and it didn't work out."

Thomas cast a knowing glance at Frump, remembering what she had said about having faith in himself. "Well," he said to the Troubadour, "at least you gave it a shot."

"Yeah," said the Troubadour ruefully, "and I might have lost my girlfriend in the bargain."

"What do you mean?" Eugene asked.

"I tried calling and writing Darlene while I was out on the road, but I haven't heard a peep out of her for months. I'm afraid she might've found somebody else while I was out gallivanting around."

"Do you still love her?" Hilda (the romantic one) wanted to know.

"More than ever. I sure did miss her while I was out there on the road." The bus was climbing Knob Hill now, approaching the little white house with the green shutters. "Just pull up there in the yard, ma'am," the Troubadour said.

The bus squealed to a stop and the Troubadour rose and gathered up his suitcase and guitar case. "It's been mighty nice meeting you folks. You're a lot of fun to be around. Charming desperadoes. Hope you all have the best Christmas ever."

Frump opened the door and the Troubadour climbed off the bus and started across the yard toward the front porch of the house. Just then, Donald lowered the window next to his seat and yelled out, "What'll you do if she won't let you in?"

The Troubadour stopped in his tracks and thought about that for a moment before he said, "Would you folks mind waiting for a minute?"

"Take your time," Frump said. "We'll wait right here."

13 ✳ Drama at Darlene's Door

The short distance between the door of the Christmas Bus and the front door of Darlene's house seemed to stretch for miles—both to the Traveling Troubadour and to all the people on the bus who watched his slow, painful journey, holding their breaths, hoping for the best, dreading the worst. If Darlene welcomed him with a big smile and open arms—well, that would make it a joyous Christmas indeed. But what if she turned him away? That would be like getting lumps of coal in your Christmas stocking. In the few short miles since the Troubadour had joined the busload, Frump and the kids had come to like him a great deal. He had an engaging talent and a winning way about him. And being out there on the road by himself all these months, struggling with disappointment— well, that was kind of like being an orphan, wasn't it?

Everybody on the bus crowded onto the side facing the house, noses pressed against the windows, watching intently as the Troubadour reached the house, mounted the steps, and set his suitcase and guitar case on the porch. He raised his hand to knock on the door, hesitated, then looked back at the bus. *Go on! Do it!* They all signaled to him. He squared his shoulders, took a deep breath, and rapped on the door. A moment passed, then several. Nothing. The Troubadour knocked again, louder this time. Then the door opened. Just a crack. And then wider.

Darlene stood there, staring out at the Troubadour. He said something. She said something. The folks on the bus couldn't hear a word of it, but they could see that there was some kind of argument going on by the way Darlene flounced her head and scrunched up her face, and they could tell by the agitated motion of the Troubadour's arms and head that he was pleading his case.

"What's she saying?" Jenny asked.

"Shhhhh!" the rest of them shushed her.

"Come on, lady!" Donald cried. "Let him in!"

And then they all started chanting, "Let him in! Let him in!"

At the house, Darlene could obviously hear the commotion on the bus, though she couldn't understand the words. She pointed at the bus. The Troubadour turned and looked back at the bus, where everybody was yelling and waving their arms, encouraging him. *Some friends of mine,* they thought they could hear him say. The Troubadour turned back to Darlene, and whatever they were agitated about went on for a moment more. And then Darlene gave an angry shake of her head and closed the door. Forcefully, with a noise that could be heard like a shot aboard the bus.

The Troubadour stood frozen in place for a long time. His shoulders slumped, his head bowed. Finally, he reached down to pick up his suitcase and guitar case.

And it was at that very moment that Donald bolted out the door of the bus, holding fast to his potted geranium plant, and sprinted toward the front porch of the house. The Troubadour had turned away and was off the porch and into the yard, headed back to the bus, when Donald sped past him in a blur of motion. The Troubadour and everyone else watched in open-mouthed amazement as Donald bounded up onto the porch and began banging his fist on the door. "Open this door, lady! You open this door!" he demanded, banging harder and harder. "Open this door right now!"

The door opened. Darlene stared out at Donald, at his geranium, at the Troubadour and the bus, and finally back to Donald. "Who are you?"

"I'm Donald. And he's," he pointed at the Troubadour, "our friend. And he's a good guy and he sings clever songs and . . . and . . . he's come all this way to see you for Christmas."

"Yeah!" Frump and the kids yelled, and there was a rowdy scramble as they all poured out of the bus and headed for the porch, everyone talking excitedly at once.

61

"Heck, lady, he loves you!" Donald said to Darlene.

"Well, I love Elmer, too," Darlene shot back, "but dang, he's unreliable."

"Elmer?" Frump and the kids said at once.

The Troubadour gave them a rueful smile. "Now you see why I call myself the Traveling Troubadour."

"Why don't you give him another chance?" Jenny demanded.

Hilda stomped her foot. "Don't you have any Christmas spirit?"

Clara said, "Let him stay till New Year's."

Eugene chimed in, "If you decide to kick him out after that, we'll take him."

"We'll give you all our Christmas presents," Louann offered, to which the others gave her a pained expression.

"You can even have my geranium," said Donald, thrusting the potted plant toward her.

"I'll tune up your car for free," Thomas said.

"I'll take care of your livestock," said Frankie with a grin.

Thomas grabbed Frankie. "Oh, no, you won't."

Frump stepped forward. "I'll bring over a fresh apple cobbler. Two!"

"So, whattaya say?" they all shouted.

"Yeah, Darlene," the Troubadour nodded vigorously, "whattaya say?"

Darlene looked thoroughly flabbergasted, befuddled, and taken aback. "Well . . ." she started to say.

But just then, they all heard the sound of a police siren, not too far away and heading in their direction at a high rate of speed.

"Omigosh, Frump," Thomas cried, "it's Sheriff Snodgrass!"

Frump turned quickly toward the bus, hustling the children ahead of her. "Good Lordy! Everybody on the bus! Quick!"

There was a mad scramble as Frump and the kids hustled aboard the bus. Frump plopped into the driver's seat and turned the ignition key as she pumped on the gas pedal furiously. *R-R-R-R-R* the engine ground in protest. *R-R-R-R-R.* "Thomas, it won't start!"

Thomas leaped from the bus and threw open the hood as the wail of the siren drew closer and closer. Frump tried again. *R-R-R-R-R. R-R-R-R-R.* "You've flooded the engine, Frump!"

Frump jumped up from the seat, arms flailing wildly as she motioned toward the door. "Everybody off the bus! Into the woods!"

They were in the process of scrambling frantically off the bus, falling over each other, when the Sheriff's car topped the rise and skidded to a stop at the edge of the road. Sheriff Snodgrass threw open the door and bounded out. "All right," he commanded in his best Sheriff's voice, "everybody just hold it right there!"

14 ✳ Caught!

Everybody froze. And Frump's heart fell so far and so hard that it landed with a thump somewhere just below her feet. Caught! All her carefully-laid plans gone awry, her swan song ending on a sour note. Yes, she knew that she was living on borrowed time as Director of the Peaceful Valley Orphanage. The Busybodies were after her hide, and they would no doubt get it, because Sheriff Snodgrass and the other members of the Board of Trustees didn't dare oppose them. And maybe the Busybodies were right—maybe she was getting too old and too soft to manage a houseful of spirited children. Maybe love wasn't enough. Maybe it was time to step aside and let a younger, more energetic, more efficiently organized person take over. She had wanted just one last hurrah—a gift of an unforgettable Christmas to these dear children. But now . . .

She made one last attempt to resuscitate her project. "Sheriff Snodgrass, I can explain. You see, we were . . . and then we picked up this . . . and the bus wouldn't . . ." her hands flew and fluttered and her tongue got all tangled around itself. The kids looked on in horror, seeing a natural disaster happening before their eyes.

"Miz Frump," said the Sheriff, hands on his hips and a scowl on his face, "I know what you're up to."

Frump stopped her blabbering and her hand went to her mouth. "Oh, dear," she said sadly.

"I thought I recognized that bus back yonder, even though you tried to disguise it with all that Christmas stuff. So I put in a call to the manager of the Hooterville Headknockers. And then I started checking around the county and found out about all these families you've got lined up. Farming your Hooligans out for Christmas."

Thomas blurted, "It was all my idea, Sheriff. I'll take the blame."

"No, Thomas, it was Miz Frump's idea. And . . . "

But the Sheriff was abruptly interrupted by the roar of an automobile engine, and they all turned to see what could only be a worse disaster than Sheriff Snodgrass catching up to them. A dull gray sedan topped the rise, and through the windshield they could see the grim face of Myrtle at the wheel, Ethel seated beside her, and Hortense leaning over from the back seat. A groan went up from Frump and the kids.

The car skidded to a stop at the edge of the road, right behind Sheriff Snodgrass's cruiser, the doors flew open, and the Busybodies erupted from the car like three volcanoes, all chattering at once, Myrtle rattling the map, all three brandishing their notebooks. They surrounded the Sheriff, chattering self-righteously at once in such angry verbal confusion that Frump and the kids could barely make out what they were saying. They could understand a word now and then: " . . . caught her red-handed . . . gallivanting . . . insubordination . . . without permission . . . reckless endangerment . . . unauthorized . . . " The Sheriff looked frantically from one to the other, wide-eyed under their assault. This went on for a minute or so, and everyone except the Busybodies could see the Sheriff's neck turning red around his collar and his eyes beginning to bulge and his ears beginning to twitch uncontrollably.

Finally, the Sheriff threw up his hands and bellowed, "Quiet!"

The Busybodies froze. From all appearances, it would seem that no one had ever told them to be quiet. They recovered after a long moment and opened their mouths to speak again. And again the Sheriff bellowed, "Quiet!"

This time, the Busybodies stayed quiet. The Sheriff turned to the rest of the crowd, hitched up his gun belt, gave a vigorous shake of his head, and said, "I was just about to say, before I was rudely . . . " (a severe glance at the Busybodies) " . . . interrupted, that I think lining up families for these young'uns for Christmas is just about the best idea Miz Frump has had in a long time."

It took a split second for that to sink in, and then Frump and the kids said, "You do?"

"Yep. A really special Christmas. I support the idea one hunnert and fifty percent. And what's more . . . " (another severe look at the Busybodies) ". . . I am of the firm opinion that Miz Frump is doing a splendid job of running the orphanage, and that she doesn't need *anybody* sticking their *noses* in her *business!*"

The Busybodies stared at the Sheriff. Hortense started to open her mouth and the Sheriff bellowed, "Anybody!"

"Yeaaaahhh!" the kids all shouted.

The Busybodies stared some more at the Sheriff, then they stared at Frump and the kids, and then they stared at each other. "Well!" they said to each other with great indignation, and then they turned on their heels and scurried briskly away to the car, which roared to life and made a screeching U-turn in the road and sped away in a cloud of dust and gravel. The folks in Darlene's yard all watched them go, and then Frump and the kids erupted in a cheer and surrounded the Sheriff, laughing and slapping him on the back. They might have raised him up on their shoulders and paraded him around the yard as they would have a football coach whose team won the big game, except that the Sheriff was a bit hefty for that.

15 ✻ Fame and Fortune

All the while, the Traveling Troubadour and Darlene had been standing on the porch, observing the rhubarb going on in the yard, so dumbfounded they couldn't speak. When the celebration had died down a bit, the Sheriff held up his hands for quiet. "Anyhow," he said, "that's not what I came out here for. I'm looking for a fellow that's known as the Traveling Troubadour."

Just as the Troubadour was about to speak, Frankie interrupted. "You don't have a warrant or anything, do you?"

"Lord, no," the Sheriff said. "A big record company is trying to locate him. They said he might be headed out here to Knob Hill."

"Why is a big record company trying to locate him?" the Troubadour asked, all curiosity now.

"He put out a song called 'Santa Wears Suspenders' or something like that."

"No," Donald spoke up, "it's 'Santa Wears Cowboy Boots.'"

"Yeah, that's it." Then the Sheriff gave Donald a close look. "How did you know?"

"Because . . . " Donald started, and then the rest of them joined in, making a grand sweep of their arms toward the porch, *that's the Traveling Troubadour!*"

Sheriff Snodgrass strode quickly to the porch and stuck out his hand. "I'm mighty proud to make your acquaintance, son. That record company says every radio station in the country is playing your song, and the records are selling like hotcakes, and . . . of course, you know all this . . . "

The Troubadour gave the Sheriff's hand a vigorous shake. "No, sir, I've been on the road.

The trucker I hitched a ride with the last few days was listening to a book on tape. Something called 'Ulysses.' I slept most of the time."

"Good grief," said the Sheriff. "Well, I'm sure glad I found you."

"But why is that record company in such an all-fired hurry to track me down on Christmas Eve?" the Troubadour asked.

"They want you in Nashville as soon as possible. They said they want to record a whole bunch of your songs. And they're lining up a national tour." The Sheriff reached in his jacket pocket and pulled out a thick sheaf of papers. "Here. . . they sent a contract by special delivery. They want you to sign it and send it back."

Quicker than a wink, Darlene snatched the contract and stared intently at the top page, her eyes going wide. "Honey, we're rich!"

"We?" the rest of them chorused.

"The Traveling Troubadour and his new bride!" Darlene gushed, giving the Troubadour's arm a honey of a squeeze as she pulled him toward the front door. "Elmer, you come on in the house, now." She called out through the open doorway, "Mama! Daddy! Elmer's here! He's staying for Christmas!"

"Really?" the Troubadour asked, astonished.

"Of course, honey-bunch," said Darlene with a big grin.

Donald grabbed the Troubadour's other arm. "Hey, what's going on here? Five minutes ago, you were trying to get rid of the guy. Now you want to marry him."

"Well," said Darlene matter-of-factly, "I think Elmer just got a whole lot more reliable."

"That record company's phone number is on the contract," said Sheriff Snodgrass. "They want you to call right away."

The Troubadour gave Darlene a squeeze. "I sure will," he assured the Sheriff.

Sheriff Snodgrass turned to Frump. "Well, I guess you need to be getting along with your deliveries." Then he turned to Thomas. "Is this old bus gonna make it?"

"I'll keep her running like a top," Thomas assured him, raising the hood of the bus and tinkering with the engine.

Frump enveloped the Sheriff in a big hug, which both surprised and pleased him. "Thank you, Sheriff," Frump said, "for everything. How can I ever repay you?"

"One of your apple cobblers ought to just about do it," said the Sheriff with a smile.

"You drop by the day after tomorrow. I'll have one with your name on it."

"I'll be there," said the Sheriff, turning now toward his cruiser. "You folks all have a Merry Christmas."

They all waved and called holiday greetings to the Sheriff as he climbed into his car and started away. As he did, he turned on the cruiser's flashing lights and siren, just for fun.

"Well now," the Troubadour said as the Sheriff's car pulled out of sight, "you folks have been mighty nice to me, so what can I do for you with all this newfound wealth I'm supposed to be getting? Anything at all. You name it."

"Anything?" Frump asked.

"Money's no object. What's fame and fortune worth if you can't share it?"

Frump looked around at her kids. At first glance, it would appear that they were all pretty needy. But Frump had surrounded them with love, and their happy, upturned faces said they were pretty wealthy after all. Then her glance fell on Thomas, bent over with his head inside the bus engine. "Thomas needs a college education," she said. "He'll be a brilliant mechanical engineer if he just gets a chance."

Thomas raised up with a jerk. "Aw, Frump . . ."

"Shoot, Miz Frump," the Troubadour said, "I'll give 'em *all* a college education."

"Now, Elmer . . ." Darlene started to protest.

But Frump was quick to seize the moment. "Done! That's the most wonderful thing I've ever heard."

Thomas closed the hood of the bus and turned to Frump. "Frump, you said that good things happen at Christmas. I guess you're right." And to the Troubadour: "There's just one other thing we need . . . " He stepped up on the porch and whispered in the Troubadour's ear.

"Done!" the Troubadour said. "Darlene, tell your folks to set one more place at the table. Miz Frump is going to be spending Christmas Day with us."

Darlene gave him a peck on the cheek. "Anything you say, honey-bunch."

"Is that okay with you?" the Troubadour asked Frump.

"I'd be delighted." Then she turned to her kids. "All right, everybody on the Christmas Bus! Let's get this show on the road!"

Frump and Thomas and the rest of the kids scrambled onto the bus. Frump closed the door and turned the ignition key. *R-R-R-R* . . . and the bus roared to life, its engine running better than ever thanks to Thomas's mechanical wizardry. They all waved to the Troubadour and Darlene, who stood arm-in-arm on the porch, watching as the bus pulled out of the yard and headed down Knob Hill toward its next stop.

And then, do you know what happened?

It started snowing.

16 ✳ What Happened After

It was a beautiful snowfall—big, white, fluffy flakes that drifted from the thick, leaden clouds overhead and fell softly on fields and woods, on town and countryside, on young and old, who dashed outside to look up with wonder and awe at the only Christmas snowfall they had ever seen, or were ever to see. It was a gracious and helpful snowfall—enough to cause the spirits to soar and the ecstasy of the holiday to fill every breast, but not so much that it impeded the progress of the Christmas Bus as it made its rounds. Frump and the orphans laughed and sang, stopping every now and then to deposit a child at a warm, loving home where carols played on the radio and the windows were bright with the dazzle of lights on the Christmas trees inside. There was joy and good cheer, love and good will. And in Frump's heart, there was a glow that outshone even the brightest decoration. When she arrived at the last house, where Thomas was to spend the night and Christmas day, he gave her the biggest hug that either of them had ever been part of. As Thomas disappeared inside the house with the happy family who were making him feel at home for the holiday, Frump felt a tear of absolute, profound joy course down her cheek. Yes, she thought to herself, she had done just fine.

Now, this is not the end of our story. Life goes on, and children grow up, and things change. That's just the way it is.

Frump stayed on as director of the Peaceful Valley Orphanage for several more years. Spirited and mischievous children came and went, and she gave each of them exactly the kind of patience, understanding, and concern they needed, even if she did still dash around, wringing her hands and crying, "It's a madhouse!" Eventually, Frump decided quite on her own that it was time to retire. By then, Clara was grown, and she took over the orphanage. She was a fine director, and when confronted with a dilemma, she would always ask herself, *What would Frump do?* Once she figured that out, she was invariably on the right track.

Sheriff Snodgrass was quickly elected as the chairman of the Orphanage Board of Trustees, replacing Hortense, who had resigned in a great huff, taking the other Busybodies with her. She and Myrtle and Ethel turned their attention to what they called "more important business," that is, doing their Christmas shopping in July, making sure their homes were spic and span, sending their husbands to the barber shop once a week, and badgering the minister of the Baptist Church over issues large and small. But they never quite got over being routed by the good Sheriff.

The Sheriff eventually retired from his post as the county's chief law enforcement officer. And guess who took his place? Frankie, who had grown up to become a solid citizen. Frankie still had a sly twinkle in his eye, though, and in his spare time he was a wild bull-rider in various rodeos.

All of the kids went to college, thanks to the generosity of Elmer, the Traveling Troubadour. And Thomas—well, he did indeed go on to win the Nobel Prize for Thing-A-Ma-Jigs. He donated his entire prize money, a quite substantial sum, to the orphanage. That, along with the generosity of the Traveling Troubadour, made it possible for every child who ever came to the Peaceful Valley Orphanage to get a college education.

Donald, who had saved the day there at Darlene's house on Christmas Eve, became a well-known horticulturalist. And what do you think he specialized in? Geraniums, of course.

Eugene, who loved leaping and jumping, became a professional skydiver and gained widespread notoriety when he parachuted into the outfield of Yankee Stadium on the opening day of baseball season. It was even more notorious because no one, especially the Yankees, knew he was going to do it.

Hilda, the romantic one, became an actress and was occasionally seen in small roles in television soap operas, where she inevitably pined for a handsome leading man.

Jenny, who was sweet-tempered and artistic, became an art teacher, and always kept her cool, even when her students spilled paints and got paste in their hair.

And Louann, who was the smallest munchkin at Peaceful Valley, enjoyed a growth spurt in her teenage years and became a fine basketball player and later the coach of a girls' high school team.

All of the orphans grew up to lead good, productive lives. And in the years after, if you asked them to what they attributed their success, they would give you one word: "Frump."

What about the Troubadour? He became a major singing star with several highly successful albums of his clever and witty songs. He got his own TV show on a major network and won a number of Grammy Awards. He and Darlene are living happily now in Las Vegas with all the little Troubadours. He performs nightly before sold-out and enthusiastic crowds, who listen to every word he sings. And he no longer calls himself the Traveling Troubadour. He's simply Elmer, because he decided that a fellow should be proud of his name, whatever it is. And Elmer is a perfectly good name.

Does all of this sound too good to be true? Well, what do you expect? It's a Christmas story. And Christmas is a time when magical things happen—when, for instance, a busload of orphans can learn that good things unfold when you open your heart to that exuberantly messy, wonderfully unpredictable, utterly joyous thing called love.

And that's what Christmas is about, isn't it?

THE END

★ ★ ★ Acknowledgments ★ ★ ★

The Christmas Bus was born in a van traveling from Denver to Breckenridge, Colorado, several years ago. It was a few days before Christmas, and the van was filled with tourists heading to the ski slopes. Except for one —a young man carrying a battered guitar case and a duffel bag. He shared his story with the rest of us: a year on the road, trying to make it as a folksinger, with a girlfriend left behind in Colorado. She was mighty upset that he went, but he just had to try. Over the year, they had lost touch. Now, he was going back. Would she be glad to see him? Maybe not. Maybe there was someone else. But he was taking the chance because he still loved her and missed her and needed her even more than his music.

He was the first passenger out of the van. It pulled up in front of a small house and he climbed out, guitar case and duffel bag in hand, and trudged up to the door. He knocked and it opened a bit, revealing a young woman. They carried on an animated, sometimes heated conversation. Those of us in the van couldn't hear, but we crossed our fingers and held our breaths and maybe even prayed a little. *Come on, lady. He loves you. Let him in.* And then she did. And we clapped and cheered and maybe even shed a tear or two. The folksinger disappeared inside with a wave, and we drove on into the night. It was Christmas, and maybe all wasn't exactly right with the world, but this sure was.

As I savored the experience, my imagination took over. The folksinger became the Traveling Troubadour and the van became a bus full of singing orphans and a warmhearted, frazzled woman who loved and took care of them and led them on the adventure of their lives. It first was a play, produced at North Carolina's Blowing Rock Stage Company under the wise and talented hand of artistic director Ken Kay. Then Lyle Baskin, who designed the set for the play, suggested that it should be a book. And he could illustrate it. So here are the story and characters in another form, brought wonderfully to life through Lyle's own imagination.

I'm indebted to Ken Kay for helping give birth to the story; to Lyle Baskin for making his special magic; to Frye Gaillard, Amy Rogers, Carol Adams and Bonnie Campbell of Novello Festival Press for giving it a whole new life. And especially to that Colorado folksinger. Wherever he is, I hope he's still in love and still making music.

★ ★ ★ NOVELLO FESTIVAL PRESS ★ ★ ★

Novello Festival Press, under the auspices of the Public Library of Charlotte and Mecklenburg County and through the publication of books of literary excellence, enhances the awareness of the literary arts, helps discover and nurture new literary talent, celebrates the rich diversity of the human experience, and expands the opportunities for writers and readers from within our community and its surrounding geographic region.

★ ★ ★ THE PUBLIC LIBRARY OF CHARLOTTE AND MECKLENBURG COUNTY ★ ★ ★

For more than a century, the Public Library of Charlotte and Mecklenburg County has provided essential community service and outreach to the citizens of the Charlotte area. Today, it is one of the premier libraries in the country — named "Library of the Year" and "Library of the Future" in the 1990s — with 23 branches, 1.6 million volumes, 20,000 videos and dvds, 9,000 maps and 8,000 compact discs. The Library also sponsors a number of community-based programs, from the award-winning Novello Festival of Reading, a celebration that accentuates the fun of reading and learning, to branch programs for young people and adults.